GEORGE UPSIDE DOWN

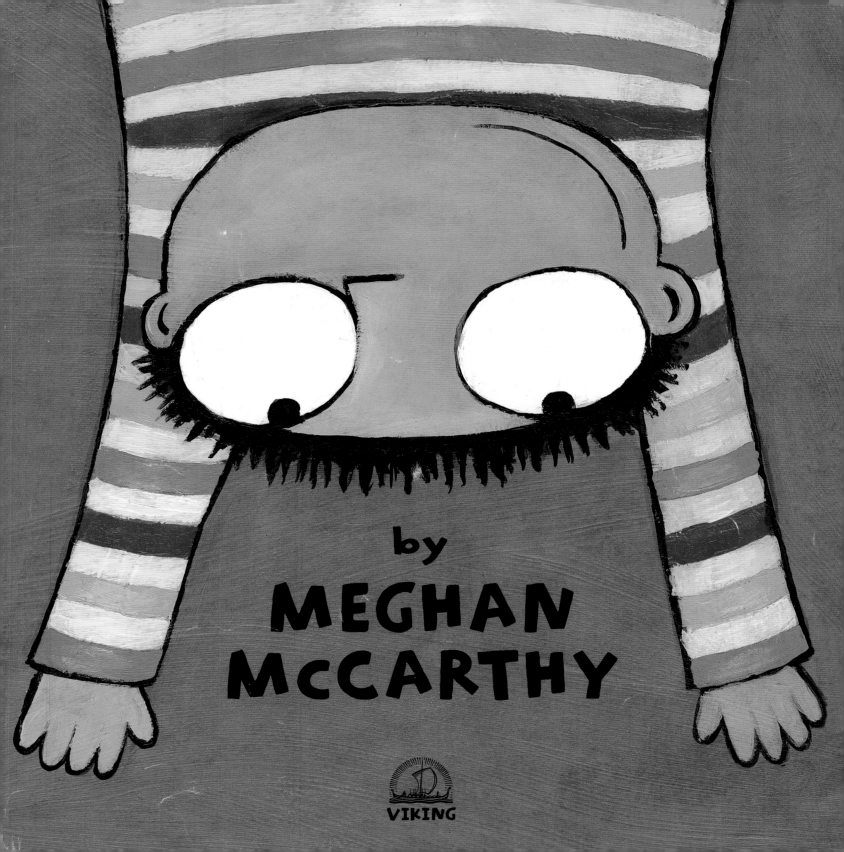

by

MEGHAN McCARTHY

VIKING

VIKING
Published by the Penguin Group
Penguin Putnam Books for Young Readers,
345 Hudson Street, New York, New York 10014, U.S.A.
Penguin Books Ltd, 80 Strand, London WC2R 0RL, England
Penguin Books Australia Ltd, 250 Camberwell Road, Camberwell, Victoria 3124, Australia
Penguin Books Canada Ltd, 10 Alcorn Avenue, Toronto, Ontario, Canada M4V 3B2
Penguin Books (N.Z.) Ltd, 182-190 Wairau Road, Auckland 10, New Zealand

Penguin Books Ltd, Registered Offices: Harmondsworth, Middlesex, England

First published in 2003 by Viking, a division of Penguin Putnam Books for Young Readers.

1 3 5 7 9 10 8 6 4 2

Copyright © Meghan McCarthy, 2003

LIBRARY OF CONGRESS CATALOGING-IN-PUBLICATION DATA
McCarthy, Meghan.
George upside down / Meghan McCarthy.
p. cm.
Summary: After George starts doing everything upside down, his parents
and teacher do the same and so he must think of something new.
ISBN 0-670-03608-0 (hardcover)
[1. Behavior—Fiction.] I. Title.
PZ7.M4784125 Ge 2003
[E]—dc21 2002011308

Manufactured in China
Set in Gill Sans
Book design by Kelley McIntyre

At the age of seven I wrote,
"My special people are Mom and Dad.
They do all sorts of stuff for me and I like it."

To my parents.
Thanks for still doing "stuff."

George likes to do many things.
But he *loves* to be upside down.

Here are a few things George likes to do while upside down. . . .

Play the trumpet

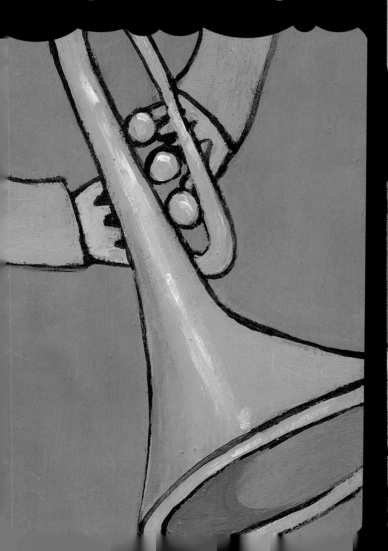

paint pictures

read books

watch TV

master the yo-yo

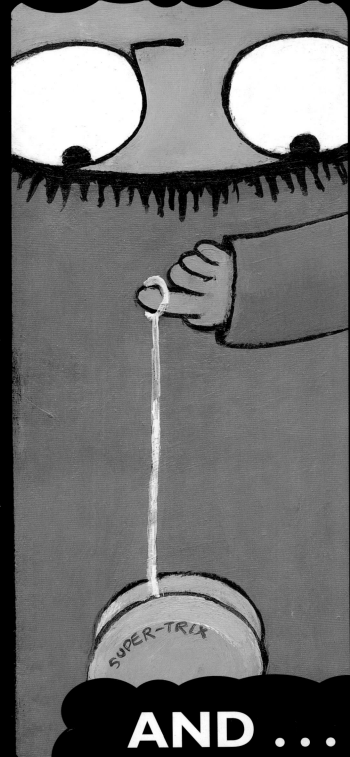

wear 3-D glasses

AND . . .

Dream!

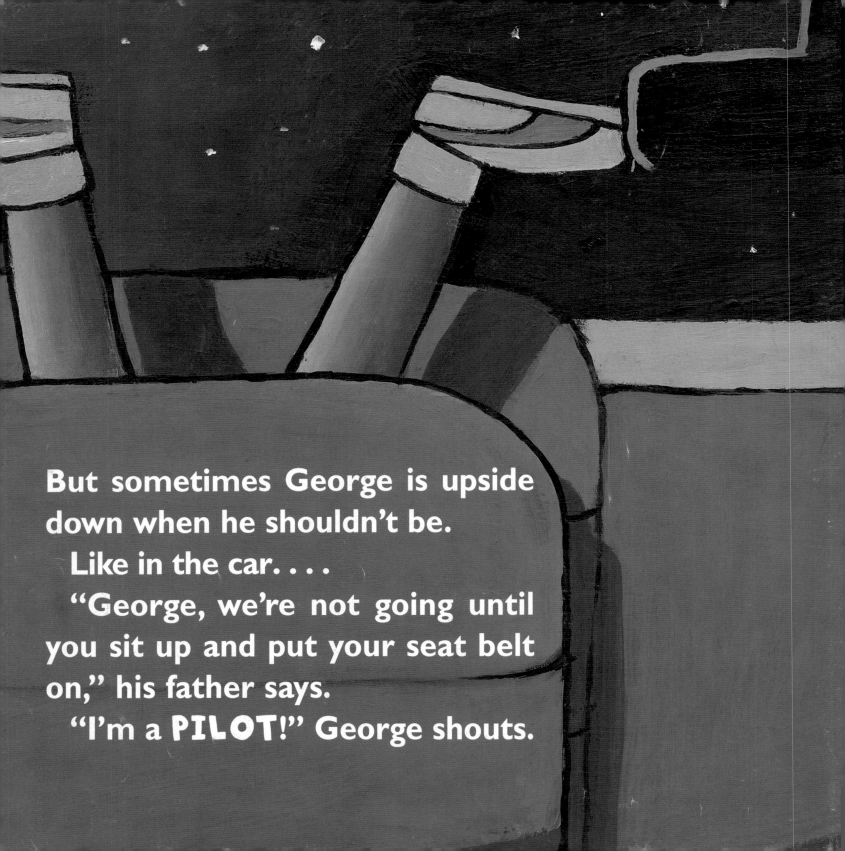

But sometimes **George** is upside down when he shouldn't be.
   Like in the car. . . .
   "George, we're not going until you sit up and put your seat belt on," his father says.
   "I'm a **PILOT**!" George shouts.

And at the dinner table. "George, stop spilling your food," his mother says.

"I'm a **DOG!**" George barks.

George does it in class, too.
"Learning must be done right side up, George," his teacher says.
"I'm a BAT!" George yells.
His teacher sends George to a private tutor so he'll learn to pay attention.

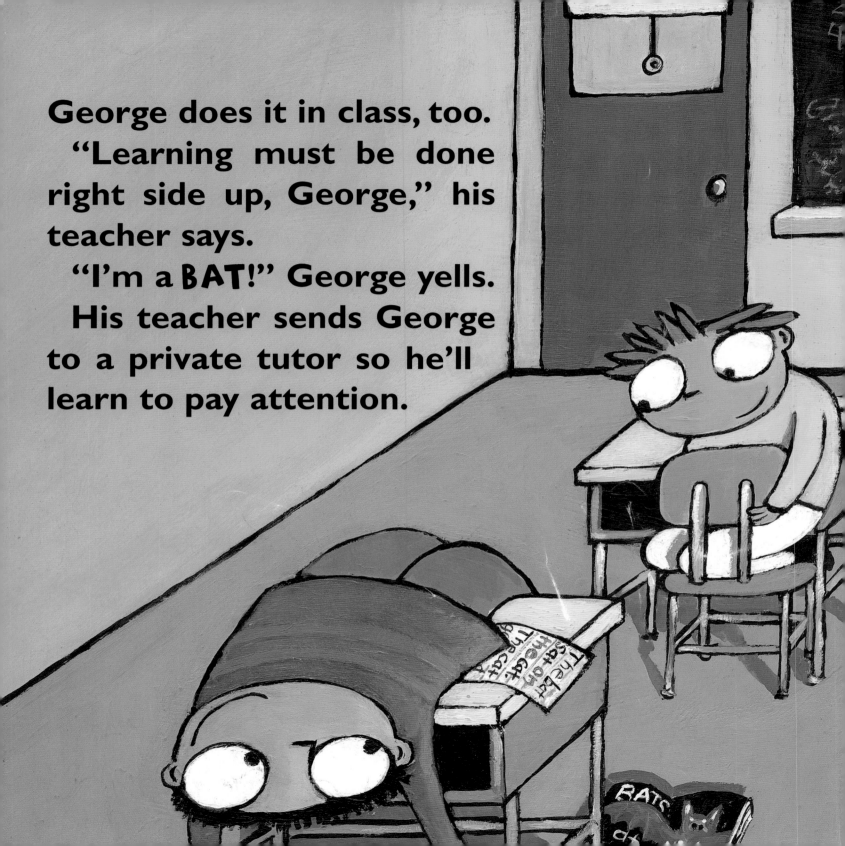

That doesn't work very well.
"You can't learn about outer space while you're upside down," his tutor says.

"I'm an **ASTRONAUT!**" George squeals. His tutor sends George to the nurse so he'll be cured.

ONLY . . .

That doesn't work either.
  "You must be right side up to get a check-up," the nurse says.
  "I'm a **SKELETON**!" George yelps.
  The nurse sends George to the principal so he'll behave.

ONLY . . .

That *definitely* doesn't work.

"You look funny upside down," George says.

The principal says . . . nothing.

The principal sends George to wait outside.
One, two, three, four, five people walk by.

The principal's door opens and shuts.
George waits.

ONLY . . .

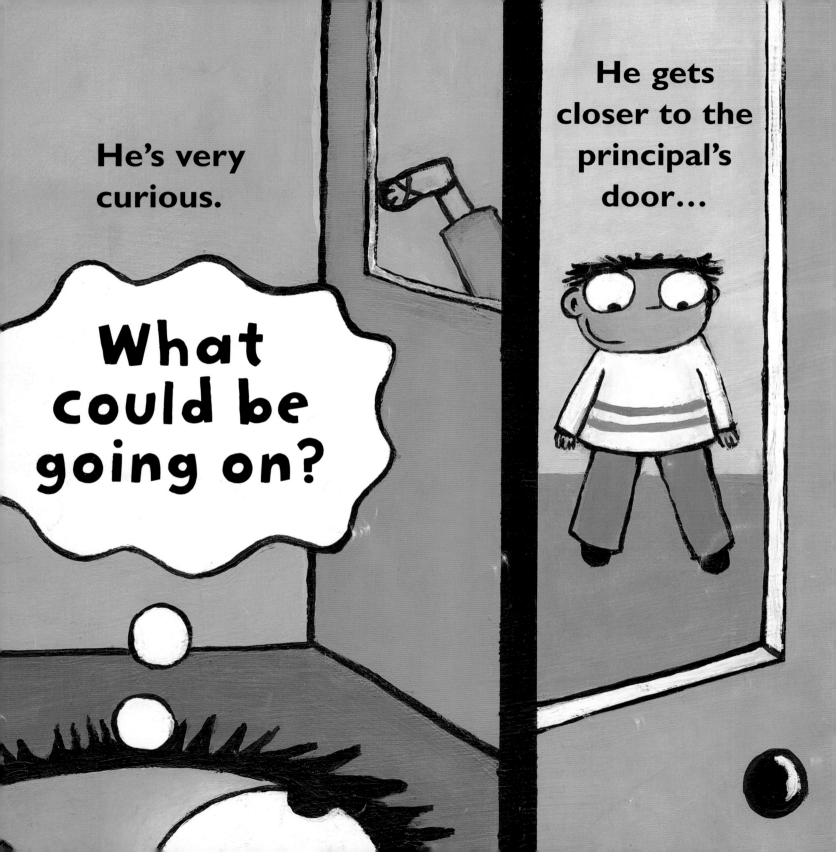

and
CLOSER . . .

and CLOSER . . .

AND THEN . . .

George GASPS.
His parents, his tutor, his teacher,

the school nurse, and the principal are all
upside down. George frowns and says . . .

Then George

LEAPS!

back to class.

not as much.

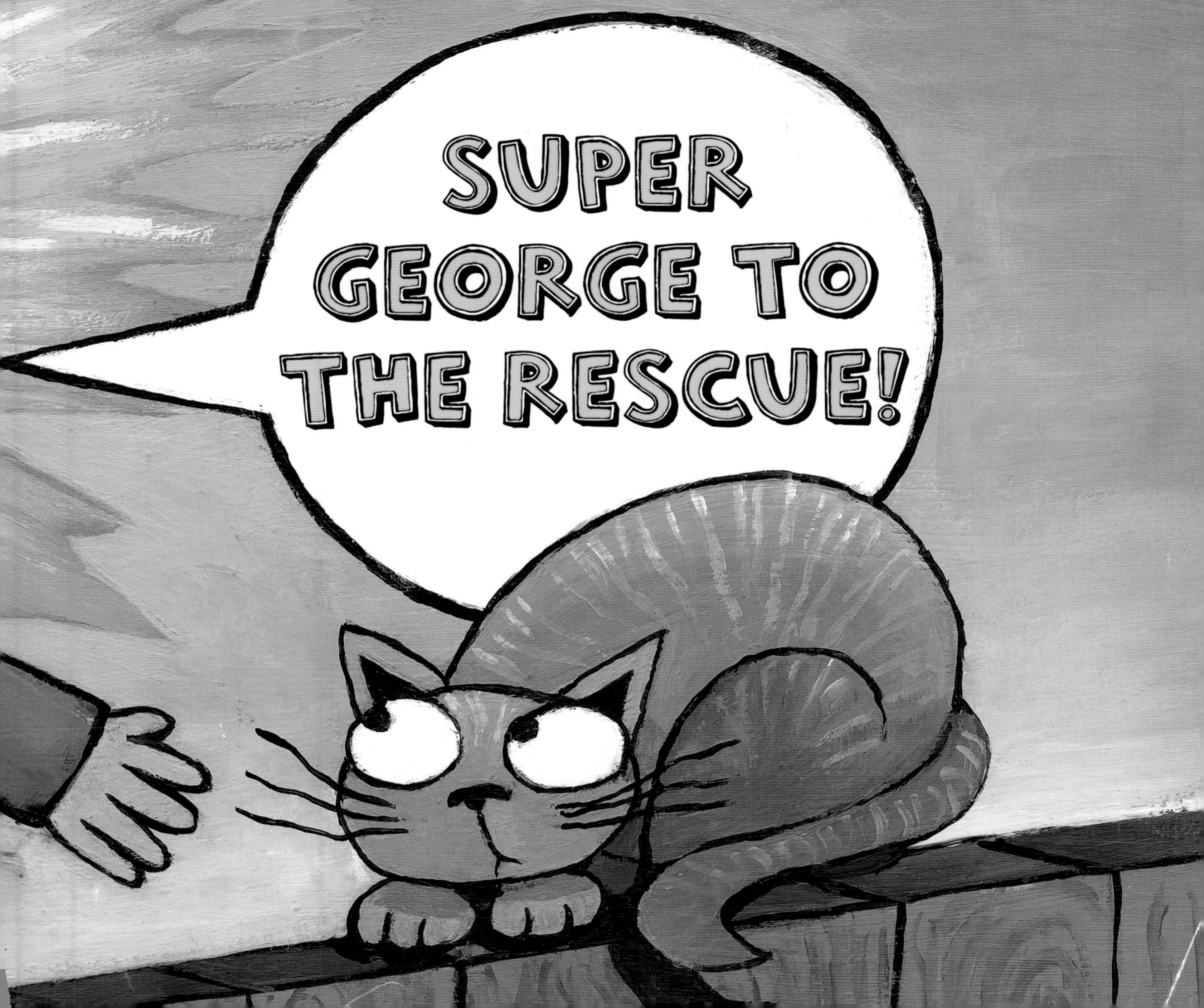